Barney Buttons &

the Secrets of Brandeland

Jan Greenwood

Copyrights © 2025 By Jan Greenwood

All Rights Reserved

No part of this book may be reproduced or transmitted in any form by any means, electronic or mechanical, including photocopying and recording, or by any information storage and retrieval system, except as may be expressly permitted in writing from the author.

Table of Contents

Chapter 1:
The Arrival on Laurel Avenue

The car slowed to a stop, and Lily pressed her face against the window, looking out at the quiet street. The chaos of Bristol was far behind them, replaced by the stillness of this old neighbourhood. The house in front of them was large, with ivy crawling up its stone walls, a mix of charm and mystery.

"This is it!" their mom said, smiling warmly. "Welcome to Nanna Jan's house."

Lily grinned. "It looks like it belongs in a fairy tale," she said, eyes wide with wonder.

Tom tilted his head. "It's big," he said, rubbing his chin thoughtfully. "But kind of spooky too."

Lily's eyes sparkled as she caught sight of the grand porch swing. "I think it's perfect."

They climbed out of the car, stretching their legs as they grabbed their bags. The air felt fresh, the scent of flowers mixing with the earthy aroma of rain-soaked dirt. It was a far cry from the smog and rush of the city.

Tom adjusted his cap. "I hope Nanna Jan's house is as cool as she says. I've always wanted to have a summer like this."

Lily nodded, a bit more hesitant than her brother. "I don't know, Tom. This place... it feels different. Like it's hiding something."

"Maybe it's hiding a secret garden," Tom teased, poking her in the side. "Come on, let's go check it out."

They walked up the stone path toward the house, and before they could even knock, the door swung open. Standing in the doorway was Nanna Jan, beaming with love and excitement.

"There you are!" she said, enveloping them both in a warm hug. "I've missed you two so much!"

"Hi, Nanna Jan!" Lily said, pulling back to look at her grandmother.

"Hi!" Tom added, his energy bubbling over.

Nanna Jan stepped aside to let them in. "Well, come in, come in! The house is waiting for you."

As they entered, the house felt both cosy and a little strange. The hallway seemed longer than it should be, and the paintings on the walls were not like the ones they'd seen before. They seemed... alive.

"Look at that," Lily whispered, pointing to a painting of a dog. To her astonishment, the dog's tail wagged as though it had been brought to life.

"Did you see that?" Lily gasped, turning to Tom. "The dog—its tail just moved!"

Tom raised an eyebrow. "You're seeing things."

"I swear it moved!" Lily insisted.

Nanna Jan, hearing the excitement, chuckled. "Oh, I see you're already noticing the little things," she said with a knowing smile. "This house is full of surprises. You'll find more magic if you look closely."

Before they could respond, the doorbell rang. "That must be the neighbours," Nanna Jan said, going to answer it. She opened the door with a flourish, revealing two very colourful figures standing on the porch.

"Well, well! What have we here?" Sherice Mrs. Kaleidos Flamingo said, her voice full of energy. She wore a large, feathery hat and a dress that sparkled with vibrant colours. "You must be the children! Welcome to the neighbourhood!"

Lily and Tom exchanged curious glances. Sherice's dress was unlike anything they'd ever seen.

"Hello!" Mr. Pontious Flamingo greeted, adjusting his enormous bow tie. "I'm Mr. Pontious, Sherice's husband. We've been waiting to meet you both."

"This is our new neighbour, Nanna Jan!" Sherice added, giving Nanna Jan an exaggerated hug. "She's told us so much about you two! Oh, we're going to have so much fun!"

"Fun?" Tom said, intrigued. "What kind of fun?"

Sherice leaned in with a conspiratorial wink. "Oh, darling, I'll tell you all about it. But first, let me tell you about the magic of this place. Laurel Avenue may look ordinary, but there's magic in every corner. And this house—well, it's just the beginning."

Lily's eyes lit up. "Magic?" she asked, her voice full of wonder. "Real magic?"

"Of course," Sherice replied with a playful smile. "This house is full of secrets. Some of them are a bit old, but you two will uncover them. I'm sure of it."

Tom was skeptical but excited. "Are we talking about a secret garden or something?"

"Oh, much more than that," Mr. Pontious chimed in, stepping forward. "You see, Brandeland isn't just a place you visit. It's a world you enter. A magical world full of creatures and wonders."

Lily gasped. "A world? Like a whole new place?"

Sherice's eyes twinkled as she nodded. "Yes, a world you can only see if you know where to look. This house—well, it's the doorway to that world. But only the brave and curious can find it."

Nanna Jan watched them carefully, a proud smile on her face. "You'll both see soon enough. But remember, you have to trust in the magic. And in yourselves."

Lily and Tom exchanged excited glances. They had so many questions, but they couldn't wait to find out more. "What do we do first?" Lily asked, bouncing on her heels.

Sherice laughed, her feathers rustling. "First, you explore. The house has so much to show you, but you have to look closely. And remember, magic isn't always where you expect it."

"Well, I'm ready!" Tom said, grinning.

"Me too!" Lily agreed, her curiosity growing by the second.

As they stepped further into the house, the air seemed to hum with excitement. It was as though something—someone—was waiting for them. They couldn't wait to see what mysteries lay ahead.

Lesson Theme: Curiosity, Change, and Exploring New Environments

Curiosity is the key to discovering new things! When you step into a new place, whether it's a new room, a new town, or even a whole new world like Brandeland, it's important to keep an open mind and be ready for surprises. Change can be exciting, and exploring new environments helps you learn more about yourself and the world around you.

As you discover new places, you might find things that are completely unexpected—things that make you stop and think, "Wow, I never saw that coming!" These surprises are what make exploring so much fun!

Exercise: "New Place Scavenger Hunt"

Sometimes, exploring means noticing the little things around you. For this activity, we want you to go on a Scavenger Hunt—but not just any scavenger hunt! This one is about the odd and interesting things you discover in a new place.

Instructions:

Pick a place: It could be a new space you're visiting, like a friend's house or a park. Or you can imagine a brand new place in your mind!

Look closely: Pay attention to everything around you— look for the unusual, the funny, the magical, or even the things that make you wonder.

Find three things: Write down or draw **three things** you find in the new space that are **interesting or odd**. It could be anything from a funny-looking chair to a hidden door, or even a place that feels like it's from a different time or world.

Explain why: Write or share why you think these things are interesting or odd. What makes them stand out? Why are they special?

Example:

Let's say you're in Nanna Jan's magical house (just like Lily and Tom). You might discover:

A painting of a dog that suddenly **wags its tail**— because the house has magical art!

A door that's always a little open, no matter how many times you close it—maybe there's something hidden inside.

A big, colourful hat on the table that **glows in the dark**—what could that mean?

Now, it's your turn! Find three things that make you go "Hmm…" and write them down, draw them, or tell someone about them!

Chapter 2:
The Bear in the Attic

Lily and Tom were standing in the attic, surrounded by old trunks and dusty furniture, when something strange caught Lily's eye—a teddy bear sitting on a forgotten shelf. It was a dusty brown bear wearing a red bowtie, and looked old, but somehow... special.

Lily: "Tom, look at this bear! Isn't it the oddest thing?"

Tom: "Huh, yeah… it's kind of... big for a teddy bear, don't you think?"

As soon as Lily picked up the bear, the most magical thing happened. The bear's eyes opened wide, and it stretched its little arms.

Barnaby "Barney" Buttons (in a jolly voice): "Well, hello there, my new friends! I'm Barnaby 'Barney' Buttons. You must be Lily and Tom, yes?"

Lily and Tom stared at the bear, their mouths wide open.

Tom: "Did—did that bear just talk?"

Lily: "I think it did!"

Barney: (laughing) "Oh, don't be so surprised! There's plenty more magic where that came from. But before we get too excited, I have a story to share with you. You see, you've just stumbled into something very special—Brandeland."

Lily's eyes grew wide.

Lily: "What's Brandeland?"

Barney: "Ah, a place full of wonder, but also a place that needs your help. But first—come closer, and I'll tell you more."

Suddenly, as if answering the call of magic itself, the attic mirror began to glow. A figure appeared in the reflection—a shimmering, golden deer with antlers that seemed to twinkle like the stars.

Brandon the Magical Deer (through the mirror): "Lily, Tom, the world of Brandeland is in great danger. You are the only ones who can help us. We need your courage to save us. Come through the mirror!"

Lily felt her heart race, but something deep inside her told her this was real, and that she needed to act.

Lily: "We have to go, Tom. This is our chance to do something big."

Tom: (nervously) "But... what if it's dangerous?"

Barney: (grinning) "Ah, the only danger is not trying! Magic is real, and you're braver than you think. Now, let's go!"

The two kids nodded, feeling the power of Barney's words. Together, they stepped toward the glowing mirror.

And then they felt it—like an invisible wall, soft but firm. They couldn't pass. It was as though the mirror itself was refusing them.

Barney: "Ah yes… I should have mentioned. This is a special kind of mirror—one that no child or animal can pass through if their heart is clouded with fear or doubt. You must clear your minds, trust yourselves, and truly believe."

Lily looked at Tom, took a deep breath, and whispered,

Lily: "We can do this."

Tom: "Okay. Let's be brave."

As they let go of their fear and opened themselves to the magic, the resistance melted away. The shadow in the mirror faded, and the portal shimmered with light.

Hand in hand, Lily and Tom stepped through the mirror—into Brandeland.

Lesson Theme: Trusting Magic, Trusting Ourselves

When we trust in the magic around us—and trust ourselves to take that first step—we unlock the power within us. Lily and Tom could have been scared or unsure, but by trusting their instincts and the magic of Brandeland, they set off on an adventure that would change their lives.

Exercise: "You're Braver Than You Think!"

Sometimes, we face things that scare us, but with a little courage, we can do things we never thought we could. For this exercise, think about a time you were scared, but you did something anyway. Maybe it was speaking in front of the class or trying something new for the first time.

Instructions:

Think of a time when you felt scared or nervous.

Draw or write about that moment. What made you nervous? What did you do, even though you were scared?

Look back at that moment and see how brave you were. You're stronger than you think!

14

Chapter 3:
The Hidden Door

With Barney leading the way, Lily and Tom followed the glowing mirror into a room that felt… different. The air shimmered with magic, and in the middle of the room stood a large, wooden door—covered in vines and golden symbols.

Barney: "This is it, the entrance to Brandeland! Just beyond this door lies a world of magic waiting for you."

The door creaked open slowly, and a rush of fresh air flooded the room. Beyond the door, a lush forest stretched out before them, filled with vibrant colours and strange, beautiful creatures. A clever fox with a bushy tail bounded up to them.

Josh Mr. Fox: (grinning) "Ah, the travellers arrive! Welcome to Brandeland! My name's Josh, and I'll be your guide through the woods."

Lily: "This place is amazing! It's like nothing I've ever seen."

Tom: (in awe) "I don't even know where to start…"

Barney: (laughing) "The best thing to do when you're in Brandeland is to start with your heart. Follow your curiosity, and magic will follow."

As they moved deeper into the forest, a shimmering figure leapt out from the nearby lake. It was a graceful dolphin, but instead of fins, it had elegant, sparkling wings.

Crystal Dolphin: (with a peaceful voice) "I'm Crystal Dolphin, and I've come to offer guidance. Sometimes the waters of emotion can be turbulent, but remember, every storm clears."

They moved toward a clearing with a marble fountain, where a strange, old phone stood. It rang with a sharp, bright sound.

Barney: "Ah, the Glug Glug Phone! That's the way to talk to Grandpa Allan."

Tom: "Grandpa Allan?"

Barney: "Yes, he's the keeper of Brandeland's secrets. He'll know what to do next."

With a deep breath, Lily stepped forward and picked up the receiver.

Lesson Theme: Wonder, Teamwork, and Magical Discovery

The adventure has only just begun! As they enter Brandeland, the children discover the importance of teamwork and wonder. By supporting each other and trusting the magical world around them, they will be able to face the challenges ahead.

Exercise: "Wonder Mapping"

Now, it's your turn to create a magical world of your own! Imagine a place full of wonders and mysteries. What kind of magical things would you like to see? Maybe it's a mountain that moves, a rainbow made of ice, or a tree that tells stories.

Instructions:

Draw a map of your magical world.

Label three wonders you'd like to visit. It could be a magical creature, a glowing tree, or even a secret path that leads somewhere amazing.

Describe each wonder: What makes it special? Why would you want to visit it?

Chapter 4:
Grandpa Allan's First Call

Lily hesitated for a moment, the receiver of the Glug Glug Phone held tightly in her hands. She could feel the magic in the air, and the weight of the moment was heavy with expectation. Her heart raced as she brought the phone to her ear.

Lily: "Hello?"

A crackling sound filled the air, followed by a voice that felt both comforting and wise, as though it had traveled through time.

Grandpa Allan: (his voice calm but serious) "Lily, Tom, it's good to hear your voices. I'm Grandpa Allan. I've been watching over Brandeland for a long time, and there's something you must know."

Tom: "Grandpa Allan? Are you—are you really him?"

Grandpa Allan: (chuckling softly) "Yes, yes I am, Tom. And you're in a place of great importance. Something dark is rising in Brandeland. The Shadow Weaver, a force of fear and confusion, is growing stronger. If we don't stop it, Brandeland will fall into darkness."

Lily exchanged a glance with Tom. Both of them felt a chill run down their spines, but something about Grandpa Allan's voice made them believe they could handle whatever came next.

Lily: "The Shadow Weaver? What can we do?"

Grandpa Allan: "You must stay brave, and trust your hearts. But there's something else you must know. The Shadow Weaver feeds on secrets—especially those that are hidden in the dark corners of our hearts. That's why you'll need to meet Princess Ellie and Princess Hollie."

Suddenly, the air shimmered, and two figures appeared before them. The first was a graceful girl with golden hair and a glowing aura—Princess Ellie. The second, a tall girl with dark, flowing hair and a regal presence—Princess Hollie. Both wore shimmering robes that seemed to reflect the light of the stars.

Princess Ellie: "We are the guardians of the Inner Garden, a sacred place where truths are kept safe. We've come to teach you about the most important thing you can know in Brandeland—how to protect yourselves from dangerous touches and secrets."

Princess Hollie: "We call it the NO GO TELL method. It's simple but powerful. Whenever someone does something that makes you feel uncomfortable, you say 'No,' move away, and tell someone you trust. Secrets like these, the ones that make you feel bad or scared, should never stay hidden."

Lily felt a sense of relief, hearing that there was a way to deal with such things.

Lily: "But… what if the person who touches us is someone we know? Someone we're supposed to trust?"

Princess Ellie: "That's the hardest part, Lily. But you must always remember—your body belongs to you. No one has the right to make you feel uncomfortable or do something that feels wrong. And if someone does, it's never your fault. The most important thing is to speak up. Tell someone you trust."

Princess Hollie: "And always remember, there are three kinds of touches: Good touch, Bad touch, and Confusing touch. A Good touch is something that makes you feel safe and cared for. A Bad touch is something that makes you feel scared or uncomfortable. And a Confusing touch is when you're not sure how it makes you feel, but it still doesn't feel right."

Lily nodded, feeling her heart settle. She knew that, no matter what happened in Brandeland, she could always speak up if something was wrong.

Tom: "So, if we feel confused or scared, we just say 'No,' and tell someone?"

Princess Ellie: "Exactly, Tom. And remember, you're never alone in this. You both have each other, and you can always trust Barney, Josh Mr. Fox, and Crystal Dolphin, too. We'll all protect you."

Suddenly, the phone's connection began to fade, and Grandpa Allan's voice came through once more.

Grandpa Allan: (urgently) "Lily, Tom—remember this. Trust yourselves. Trust the magic around you. And when the Shadow Weaver comes, you'll need to be strong. You can do this."

The connection ended with a soft click. Lily and Tom stood there, processing everything they had just learned. They knew this was only the beginning of their adventure, but now, they felt more prepared.

Lesson Theme: Body Safety and Boundaries

Lily and Tom had just learned one of the most important lessons they would ever hear in Brandeland: how to protect themselves and set clear boundaries. Trusting their feelings, understanding the difference between good and bad touch, and knowing when to speak up are essential skills that will help them on their journey.

Exercise: "Safe Circle Activity"

Now, it's time for you to create your own Safe Circle! A Safe Circle is made up of the people you can trust and talk to, no matter what. These are the people who make you feel safe, loved, and understood. It's important to know who is in your Safe Circle so that you can always reach out when you need help.

Instructions:

Draw a circle on a piece of paper.

Write the names of trusted people inside the circle. These might be your family members, teachers, friends, or anyone who makes you feel safe.

Think about a time when you talked to someone in your Safe Circle. How did it make you feel? What did they do to help you feel better?

Reinforce: "Good Touch / Bad Touch / Confusing Touch"

Good Touch: A touch that makes you feel happy, safe, and loved—like a hug from your parents or a pat on the back from a friend.

Bad Touch: A touch that makes you feel scared, uncomfortable, or hurt—like being pinched or touched in ways that don't feel right.

Confusing Touch: A touch that makes you feel unsure, confused, or uncomfortable, but you don't know exactly why—like someone touching you in a way that makes you question how you feel.

Chapter 5:
The Weaver Stirs

The forest grew quiet. Too quiet.

Even the rustling leaves had stilled, as if the entire world was holding its breath. A faint, shadowy mist began curling through the trees like smoke, whispering secrets as it passed.

Barney's ears perked up.

"Something's not right," he murmured.

Tom looked around, uneasy. "Where are all the birds?"

Then Lily opened her mouth to speak, but no sound came out.

She tried again. Nothing.

Her voice was… gone.

Lily clutched her throat in confusion, her eyes wide. "Mmm!" she tried to cry out, but it was like the air itself refused to carry her words.

Suddenly, a cold wind blew past them, and with it came a hiss of laughter—dry, empty, and cruel.

The Shadow Weaver.

A swirling black shape moved between the trees like a wisp of smoke in a bottle, its edges constantly changing. From its centre, two glowing eyes blinked open, locking onto Lily.

Barney stepped in front of her. "It's him," he growled. "The one Grandpa Allan warned us about."

Tom reached for Lily's hand. "Lily—what do we do?"

Barney turned to her, his voice firm. "The only way to break his spell is to remember your power. You have a voice, Lily. You just have to use it."

The Shadow Weaver laughed again, louder this time, growing bolder with each second Lily stayed silent.

Lily closed her eyes. Her chest tightened. She wanted to scream, to cry, to fight—but nothing came.

With a surge of courage, Lily remembered what Princess Ellie had said.

"Your body belongs to you. No one has the right to make you feel scared."

Lily took a deep breath and, from somewhere deep inside her, shouted, "NO!"

Her voice rang out like a thunderclap.

The mist recoiled instantly. The Shadow Weaver shrieked and stumbled back, its shape flickering.

"NO!" she shouted again, stronger this time.

The forest responded. The wind picked up. A great roar echoed in the distance.

From the edge of the woods came a figure—bold and golden with a shining mane.

Tora the Lion.

He leapt into the clearing, landing with a thunderous roar that shook the ground beneath their feet.

Tora's deep voice boomed: "You did it, Lily. That's how you protect your magic—by speaking up. Never forget that."

The Shadow Weaver hissed and melted back into the mist, disappearing—for now.

Lily's voice was back. Her heart was racing, but she felt lighter. Stronger.

Tom hugged her. "That was awesome."

Barney beamed. "Told you. You're braver than you think."

Lesson Theme: Using Your Voice to Protect Yourself

Just like Lily, we all have a voice that's strong and powerful—even when it doesn't feel that way. Speaking up when something feels wrong is one of the bravest things you can do. Saying "NO" helps break the silence and keep you safe. You are allowed to protect yourself, and your voice is a superpower.

Exercise: 🗣 "NO GO TELL" Practice

Let's practice what to do if someone makes you feel uncomfortable, confused, or scared.

Instructions:

NO – Practice saying "NO" in a strong, clear voice.

Try it in front of a mirror or with a trusted adult.

GO – Where would you go to feel safe?

Draw or write about the safe places in your life—your room, a teacher's classroom, a neighbour's house.

TELL – Who are your trusted grown-ups?

Make a list or draw pictures of people you can talk to—parents, teachers, coaches, or friends' parents.

30

Chapter 6:
Secrets and Shadows

Barney led them to a mossy clearing, where a crooked tower of rainbow-coloured bricks jutted up from the earth.

"This," he said, "is the Patchwork Library."

Tom blinked. "A library? Out here?"

Barney nodded. "But not just any library. This one holds every feeling, memory, and truth that's ever been hidden.

Some of them are real, and some are just reflections of what we think is true."

As they stepped closer, the entrance uncurled like a fern, revealing a long, dark hallway. Guarding the doorway was a shimmering snake with emerald eyes and a wise, toothy grin.

"Welcome, welcome," hissed Steve Slithery Snake, coiled on a stack of ancient scrolls. "To enter, you must answer a riddle. If you fail, the shadows may trick you…"

He slithered down to eye level.

"I am what you feel but cannot see.

I ride your thoughts and make you flee.

But name me clear, and I will pass—

A storm, a breeze, a looking glass.

What am I?"

Lily thought for a moment. "...An emotion?"

Steve's eyes twinkled. "Well done."

With a nod, he let them pass.

Inside, the Patchwork Library shimmered with thousands of tiny mirrors stitched into the walls. Instead of books, the shelves held glowing jars filled with swirling colours—memories, feelings, whispers of old secrets.

But as the children walked deeper, the mirrors began to whisper.

"You're not brave enough."

"You should have known better."

"No one will believe you."

"It was your fault."

The voices were cold and sneaky. They sounded like thoughts Lily had tried to ignore. She felt a heavy lump form in her chest.

Tom's shoulders slumped. "Why are they saying these things?"

Barney frowned. "Because the Patchwork Library doesn't just show what's real. It also reflects the shadows we carry."

Lily stepped toward one of the mirrors. Her reflection stared back—but it didn't smile. It looked ashamed. Small. Afraid.

Tears welled up in her eyes.

Just then, a shimmer lit up the room. The temperature changed—softer, calmer—and from the ceiling above, a ripple of water flowed down, forming the graceful figure of Crystal Dolphin.

Her gentle voice echoed like waves.

"Feelings aren't bad. They are messages. But when we don't name them, they twist into shadows."

She hovered beside Lily. "What are you feeling, right now?"

Lily sniffled. "I… I feel sad. And kind of mad. And confused."

Crystal nodded. "Good. That's truth. Say their names. Let them be seen."

Tom spoke up too. "I feel... scared. But I also feel like I want to protect my sister."

The mirrors flickered—and began to soften. The harsh voices faded, replaced by a warm hush.

"You are not your fears," Crystal said. "You are the one who feels them. And that means you are also the one who can let them go."

Barney wiped a tear from his fur. "Never underestimate a child who learns to name what they feel. That's real magic."

They left the library quietly, but stronger. The path behind them shimmered with colour now—not just shadows, but the full spectrum of emotion.

Lesson Theme: Naming Emotions and Self-Acceptance

Everyone feels big, sometimes messy emotions—sadness, anger, confusion, fear. That's okay. What matters is learning to name what we feel, so it doesn't have to stay hidden or grow into something heavier. When we speak our truth, the shadows shrink.

Exercise: "Feelings Mirror"

🗩 Let's create a magical mirror of your own—a place to reflect your feelings honestly and proudly.

Instructions:

Draw a mirror on a piece of paper. It can be any shape—round, heart-shaped, star-shaped, whatever feels right!

Inside the mirror, draw faces or write down words for different emotions you've felt recently. Examples: happy, nervous, excited, left out, proud, embarrassed.

Add colours or designs that match those feelings. Blue for calm, red for anger, yellow for joy—anything that helps you express it!

🌈 Remember: All feelings are welcome. The goal isn't to hide them—it's to understand them.

Chapter 7:
Nanna Jan Knows More Than She Shows

Lily and Tom stepped into a quiet glade where moonlight fell in silver ribbons. To their surprise, Nanna Jan was already there, standing by a tree that shimmered like crystal.

"Nanna Jan?" Lily whispered. "How did *you* get here?"

Nanna Jan smiled, her eyes warm with knowing. "This isn't my first time in Brandeland," she said gently. "I came here when I was your age. Back then, I was scared to speak my truth—but this place helped me find my courage."

She knelt beside them. "Each magical friend you've met—Josh, Sherice, Brandon, even Steve—they're more than just characters. They each carry something children need: courage, joy, peace, honesty. I found pieces of myself through them… just like you are now."

She placed her hand over Lily's. "And just like Brandeland found me, it's found you. You're exactly where you need to be."

Lesson Theme: Trusting Adults and Sharing Your Truth

Sometimes we carry secrets because we're afraid of what might happen if we tell. But sharing your truth with someone you trust can help you feel stronger and more free. You're never too small or too scared to speak up—there's always someone who will listen and help.

Exercise: 🎬 "Story Sharing Time"

Let's take a quiet moment to reflect.

Think about a time when you kept something to yourself because you were afraid, confused, or didn't know what to say. Maybe it was something that made you sad, scared, or even embarrassed.

Instructions:

Write it down or draw it in a private journal or on a piece of paper.

Or share it anonymously with a trusted adult if you feel ready.

Then write or draw how it felt when you finally shared it—or imagine how it might feel to let it out.

💡 Remember: Sharing your story doesn't make you weak. It makes you wise and brave—just like Nanna Jan.

Chapter 8:
The Threadlings' Trap and the Truth Spell

Lily and Tom stumbled into a clearing of twisted vines and tangled roots. All around them, tiny voices cried out.

"Help us! Unravel the knot!"

Brandon the Deer stepped forward gently, nose twitching. "The Threadlings," he said, nodding solemnly. "They're caught in the Weaver's spell. We must free them."

The Threadlings were no larger than dandelion fluff, with silver limbs and glowing eyes. They were trapped in silky webs that pulsed with dark magic.

Just then, a shimmer of gold swept across the clearing. Princess Hollie floated down, her long hair glinting like sunlight on water.

"I can help," she whispered. With slow, graceful motions, she combed her golden hair through the threads, unweaving the spell strand by strand.

The air grew lighter with each freed Threadling.

Ellie stepped forward, raising her hands. A glowing bridge stretched out before them, leading straight to the Loom of Truth. "The path is ready," she said.

As the last of the Threadlings untangled, they gathered around Lily.

"For your bravery," they chimed, their voices like wind chimes in a breeze. They held out a red dress, stitched from their own threads and woven with a magic shield. "It will protect your voice and your courage."

Lily placed her hand over her heart. "Thank you," she said, her voice strong.

But something strange began to happen.

The colours of Brandeland began to fade—slowly, like paint washing away in rain. Barney's steps slowed. The Glug Glug Phone at his belt started to flicker and crackle.

Tora the Lion stood tall, his mane glowing like fire. "It's time," he roared. "The Truth Chant must begin!"

Josh Mr. Fox and Mr. Pontious Flamingo appeared beside him, lighting a tall lantern filled with golden light.

Each character stepped forward, voice trembling with honesty.

"I was afraid to say I missed my old forest," whispered Brandon.

"I thought I wasn't brave enough to protect anyone," said Princess Hollie.

"I worried no one would like me if I told the truth," said Josh softly.

Then it was Lily's turn.

She took a deep breath. "I was scared to speak up when I felt small. But I'm not small anymore."

Tom stepped beside her. "I thought I had to be strong all the time. But I've learned that asking for help is strong too."

The tapestry above them shimmered—and then glowed, golden threads weaving through every name and every truth.

Suddenly, a shadow slithered toward them.

The Shadow Weaver.

"I offer you silence," it hissed, "and forgetting. You'll never feel pain again."

But Lily stood firm. "We choose truth."

Together, led by Nanna Jan, Ellie, Steve Snake, Crystal Dolphin, and Brandon the Deer, they raised their voices in a powerful chant.

"Truth is light, and light will grow.

Through the heart, we let it flow.

In our words, in what we see,

Truth will set our spirits free!"

The tapestry burst with golden light.

Barney glowed brighter than ever before. He rose to full life, smiling wide, no longer just a guide—but a protector of all truth.

The Weaver howled and shrank into a silver thread, sealing itself in the deepest corner of the Loom.

Brandeland stilled.

Soft winds rustled trees. Water glistened. Peace returned.

Each friend approached Lily and Tom.

Brandon gave them a gleaming horn. "Blow it when you need courage."

Then he handed them a tiny glowing seed. "Plant this when you need truth."

Nanna Jan cupped their hands. "You'll always find a path back. You just have to believe."

Lesson Theme: Carrying lessons forward

Even when stories end, truths stay with us. Carry them in your heart—they will guide you when things feel dark.

Exercise: My Brave Truth

Draw or write one truth that makes you feel strong or free.

Epilogue:
One More Ring

Back in the city, Lily sat cross-legged on her bed, Tom fiddling with a paper aeroplane.

Then—brrring!

The Glug Glug Phone rang.

But it wasn't the same one.

A new one sat blinking on the windowsill, shiny and silver, like a brother to the first.

Lily picked it up slowly.

"What new adventure is about to begin?" she whispered.

Bonus Prompt: "If You Could Call Grandpa Allan…"

Write or draw what you would say or ask if you had one magic phone call.